Bed
Races
and
Cheese
Chases

Bed Races

Races

and

Cheese

Chases

Teresa Heapy

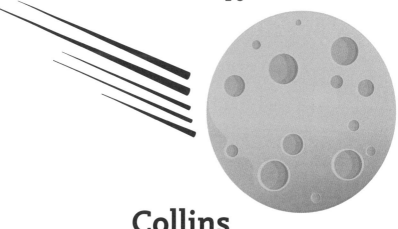

Collins

Contents

Bonus
Quirky competitions you've never heard of!

When you think of **competitions** and **championships**, you may think of the **Olympics**. However, right now, people around the world are training for some quirky competitions. These include:

- Chess Boxing involves **contestants** playing four minutes of chess and three minutes of boxing.

- There's a Cockroach Chasing competition in Australia.

- There's the World Stone Skimming Championship in Scotland.

- In the US, there is a Chilli Pepper-Eating contest, a Fantasy Hair Styling competition and a Frog Jumping Competition. There's also a Rock, Paper, Scissors championship!

- There are various championships in the UK, including Toe Wrestling, Teapot Racing, Egg Throwing, Nettle Eating, Worm Charming, Welly Wanging and Pancake Racing.

Right, are you ready to find out more? On your marks, get set – let's go!

Bonus
Championship map

Punkin' Chunkin'
Championships
(Delaware, US)

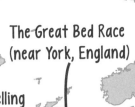

The Great Bed Race
(near York, England)

World Bogsnorkelling
Championships
(Wales)

The Cooper's Hill
Cheese Roll
(Brockworth, England)

Air Guitar World
Championships
(Oulu, Finland)

Human Tower
Competition
(Tarragona, Spain)

CHAPTER 1

The Terrific Human Tower Competition

Every two years, there is a competition to make the biggest human tower in Tarragona, Spain. Teams make towers of people which are up to ten people high. I guess you might be thinking that a tower involving just ten people would be seriously wobbly. But this is not a tower of just ten people. It involves many, many people, bracing together to allow other people to stand on top of them. The tower can be up to eight metres high and be made up of hundreds of people!

The towers require lots of bravery and planning by teams of people. The towers **symbolise** togetherness and **perseverance**, as people really have to rely on each other.

Fact!
The human towers are called castles in Catalan.

How long has it been going on?

The first tower was recorded in 1712 – that's over 300 years ago! They became more popular around the 1960s and 1970s, but to begin with, only men took part. When women started to join in, the towers began to get taller and taller. This is because women generally weigh less than men, which allows more people to be held up on top of each other.

How is a tower made?

First, the base, or the **pinya** is formed. This can be a wide web of people, supporting each other to make a firm foundation. They also form a safety net if anyone falls. Sometimes this pinya can be several hundred people on its own!

pinya

After the big base, there are usually about five layers of other people, with four to six people in each layer. This makes a huge, swooping column.

Then one final person climbs right to the very top. This person is usually a small, very brave child, wearing a special crash helmet.

A band plays while the towers are being made.
There are special tunes to accompany
the building of specific parts of the tower.
The people in the pinya cannot look up to see
what is happening above them, so the music
helps them to know what is going on.

The band uses traditional instruments which are
a bit like an oboe or clarinet, and the "timbal",
which is a special drum.

When most of the tower has been built, a hush usually comes over the spectators. They know they are at the very final (and one of the most dangerous) stages of building the tower.

The rest of the people climb up into their places as quickly as possible. This is to limit the strain on the people in the pinya at the bottom.

Finally, the child climbs into place at the very top and raises a hand in the air.

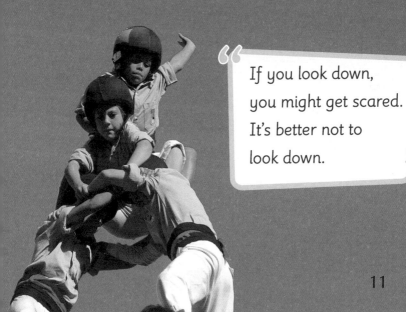

If you look down, you might get scared. It's better not to look down.

Everyone cheers! Then they all climb down carefully. This is probably the most risky part of the whole process.

The motto of the tower-climbers

Strength – they have to be strong, especially those at the base of the tower.

Balance – they all need a good sense of balance.

Courage – especially the young children who climb to the top!

Good judgement – all the tower-climbers need to be careful and sensible. They also need time to plan and practise.

"When you are close to a tower, it's like being close to a beating heart, going "Boom, boom, boom!""

Each team is dressed in a specific colour.

Up to 11,000 spectators come to watch and cheer on the teams. Ambulances are ready in case of accidents. It is a scary and precarious thing to do!

Sometimes people fall from the tower and can be seriously hurt. But everyone looks after each other. It is an exhilarating experience and an honour to take part!

Not to be tried if ...
you're afraid of heights.

CHAPTER 2

The Cracking Cheese Roll Race

Do you like racing? Do you like cheese?

Then the amazing annual Cooper's Hill Cheese Roll race is for you!

It consists of rolling a big cheese down a hill, and running after it! It's as simple as that.

The problem is the hill. It's a seriously steep hill, the sort of hill you *fall* down, rather than *run* down! Coopers Hill is 183 metres long, and the race goes along 100 metres of it.

very steep!

100 metres long

It's not the obvious place to
run down to catch a rolling cheese.

Where is it?

Cheese rolling happens annually at Cooper's
Hill, near a small town called Brockworth, near
Cheltenham, in England.

How did it start?

The first race was a very long time ago, so nobody knows exactly how it began – or indeed *why* it began. Some people say that it was all to do with claiming rights to graze sheep around Cooper's Hill.

There's a letter to the town crier in 1826 about cheese rolling, but people think it started way before that – at least 600 years earlier.

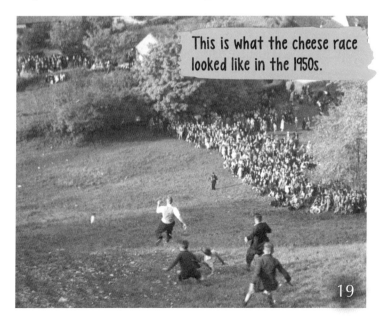

This is what the cheese race looked like in the 1950s.

19

What happens?

At the top of Cooper's Hill, the Master of Ceremonies (who is called the Master of Cheese!) releases a wheel of cheese which weighs 3.63 kilograms. Just before he lets go of the cheese, he says the following rhyme:

"One to be ready!
Two to be steady!
Three to prepare!
And four to be off!"

The Master of Cheese releases the cheese! It's protected with tape round the sides and decorated with ribbons.

The rolling cheese hurtles down the hill. It gets a one-second start before it is closely followed by a swarm of runners! The runners set off, chasing after the cheese, but as the hill is very steep, they pick up so much speed that they can fall over as they rush towards the cheese. The first runner to get to the bottom of the hill wins the contest. And the big wheel of cheese!

Can anyone enter?

At first, it was only people in the village
of Brockworth who were allowed to enter.
Now, anyone from all over the world
can take part. Winners have come from
Canada, Australia, New Zealand and Nepal.
The contestants can wear whatever they like,
but some choose to wear fancy dress.

Nearly everyone's clothes end up getting muddy or ripped, so it's best not to wear your best outfit!

Some people manage to stay on their feet. Others travel down less elegantly. There's a lot of falling over!

Some go head over heels, or cartwheeling. There are paramedics waiting at the bottom of the hill, just in case. And a lot of hay bales, to prevent runners from tumbling down into the nearby cottages.

There are many races throughout the day: three races for men and one for women. There's also an uphill race for children, going from the bottom to the top of the hill. Flo Early first won the women's cheese-rolling race when she was 17 years old, and she went on to win it a record-breaking four times! She even had a television documentary made about her.

Flo dislocated her collar bone and broke her ankle while racing. She loves the race! But she's not doing it again.

24

Just how dangerous is it?

Cooper's Hill is muddy, it's steep and it's covered in nettles. There are usually quite a number of injuries. In 2009, it was cancelled due to concerns about health and safety, but swiftly returned in 2011. It was cancelled again in 2020–21 due to the pandemic, although the cheese was still rolled down the hill on its own, to maintain the tradition! The race was back up and rolling again in June 2022.

Not to be tried if ...

you're not keen on potentially hurting yourself.

CHAPTER 3

The Amazing Air Guitar World Championships

The competitors in the Air Guitar World Championships don't play guitars. They just *pretend* to play one really well! They mime playing a guitar in an exaggerated way – as if they are strumming a real guitar. They usually do this to a loud rock song, with lots of acting, amazing costumes and some fantastic dancing. They can make you think that they are playing guitar up in the air, or even behind their head!

They just need to match their miming with the song that's playing and entertain their audience with their brilliant technique!

Look at these contestants. They are miming their guitar playing and doing it with flair!

How did it start?

The Air Guitar Championships started in 1996, and are **accessible** to everyone, whatever their age. You don't even need to own a guitar, and anyone can try it!

The most important rule is:
You can use an electric or **acoustic** guitar …
but it must be invisible!

Nanami "Seven Seas" Nagura, Air Guitar World Champion 2018 in Oulu, Finland

Justin "Nordic Thunder" Howard was the 2012 air guitar world champion. He can play the real guitar, or as he calls it the "there-guitar", but says he's much better at air guitar.

"That is the stupidest thing ever. I want to be the best in the world at that.

Nordic Thunder

Where is it?

The World Air Guitar Championships takes place in Oulu, Finland. Although some of the contestants may look a bit scary, it's a good-natured contest which is a "celebration of love and peace". The reward they seek is "to be the master of Air and leave the stage with the shiniest trophy".

There's no charge to watch the Championships, so the audience gets in free to watch a fabulous show.

What happens?

Contestants have to play two songs, each lasting 60 seconds. This includes:

- one song of their choice

- one song chosen by the judges, which the contestants first get to hear just before they go on stage.

For the first song in particular, creating some drama is important. Contestants need to tell a unique story with a beginning, middle and end. They can also plan out a fantastic dance routine.

Improvisation is really important for the second song, because contestants have only just heard it and won't get a chance to **rehearse** it. This means that they need to take a chance, and do what they think is best, live on stage!

There are many spectacular costumes, including hats, capes, glitter, jumpsuits, wigs and make up. There's a lot of leaping, jumping, dancing and knee-sliding.

There are quite a few sprained ankles and sore knees along the way, too! At the end of the night, EVERYONE plays air guitar together!

How is it judged?

The guitarists are judged by a **jury**, made up of performers, including real guitarists!

The jury has to consider these things:

- Does it look as if the contestant's hands are in the right place on their invisible guitar?

- Did the audience enjoy it? How loud was the cheering and clapping? How spectacular was the performance?

- The "airness" of the competitor!
  (Don't go looking for "airness" in the glossary as it's not an actual word. Except in the Air Guitar Championships, of course! It means making people forget someone's pretending to play a guitar, and simply enjoy their brilliant performance.)

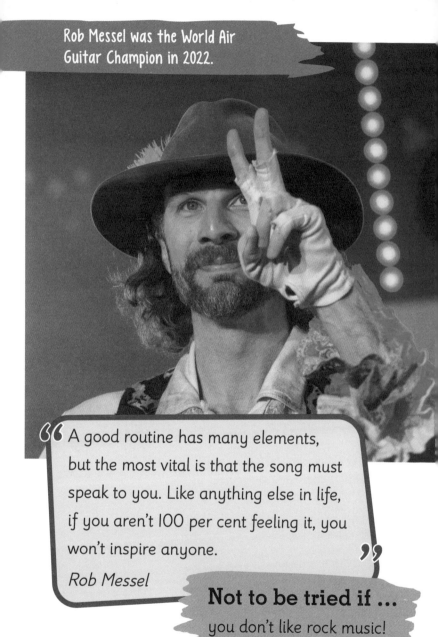

Rob Messel was the World Air Guitar Champion in 2022.

"A good routine has many elements, but the most vital is that the song must speak to you. Like anything else in life, if you aren't 100 per cent feeling it, you won't inspire anyone.

Rob Messel

Not to be tried if …
you don't like rock music!

CHAPTER 4

The Brilliant Bogsnorkelling World Championships

Now this sounds great, doesn't it?
Putting on flippers and a **snorkel** …

… getting ready and jumping into …

… a muddy, narrow trench of water!

Yes, it's time to dive into the annual Bogsnorkelling World Championships!

You heard right.
It's the Bogsnorkelling Championships.

Where are the Bogsnorkelling Championships?

The annual World Championships take place on bogland in Wales at the end of August. They started in 1986. Competitors come from all over the world. Other bogsnorkelling competitions take place in Australia, Ireland and Sweden.

What is a bog?

A bog is an area of wetland (meaning, literally, "land that is wet"), which has a lot of peat. Peat consists of a large quantity of dead plant material, including lots of moss. It's very **fertile** – and very, very wet.

Peat bogs are a brilliant **habitat** for a wide range of animals, plants and fungi. Bogs are good for the environment because the plants in them **decompose** slowly. People aren't allowed to build on them because they host so many different sorts of wildlife.

Special care is taken not to damage the bogs at the Bogsnorkelling Championships. Two very narrow trenches were dug in 1986, and these are reused year after year.

There are two trenches, so that two competitors can swim at the same time without everyone having to wait to use the same trench.

length: 55 metres

snorkel

What are the rules?

Competitors have to swim down one of the trenches. They must then touch the post at the end of the trench, turn and swim back. They swim 110 metres in total. They must not take more than two minutes to swim the first length. If they are slower, they can't complete the second length.

Competitors have to swim using "doggy paddle", which means moving your hands and kicking your feet to **propel** you through the water.

They are not allowed to use any other swimming strokes!

Competitors must also use a snorkel.

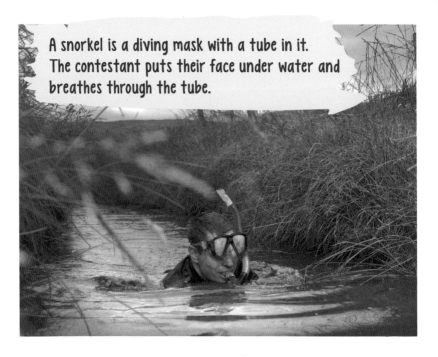

A snorkel is a diving mask with a tube in it. The contestant puts their face under water and breathes through the tube.

What does it feel like?

Usually, snorkelling is done in warm, tropical waters, looking at beautiful fish! In bogsnorkelling, all you can see is brown water! It's icy cold, the competitors' goggles get so muddy it's almost impossible to see, and the trench is filled with reeds and a very special, gluey sort of mud.

With legs kicking, contestants have to propel themselves through the peaty, smelly bog-water. They look up now and then and keep going as fast as they can, cheered on by the crowd.

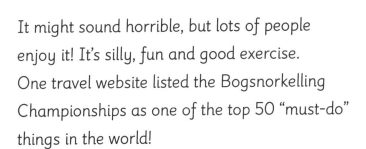

The taste is like you've washed potatoes in some water, and then you try and drink that water. It's not pleasant.

Keith Rothwell, competitor

It might sound horrible, but lots of people enjoy it! It's silly, fun and good exercise. One travel website listed the Bogsnorkelling Championships as one of the top 50 "must-do" things in the world!

Fancy dress is **optional**, but encouraged. Some people just wear a hat. Some people go a bit further.

> Part of the fun is making a fool out of yourself.
>
> *Bob, event organiser*

Awards are given out for the fastest man and woman in different categories. And it's not just adults who compete. In 2002, a 15-year-old won the world prize in 1 minute and 45 seconds. Everyone receives a medal shaped like a newt.

Neil Rutter has won the Bogsnorkelling World Championships three times. He holds the Guinness World Record for the fastest time of 1 minute 18.82 seconds.

Not to be tried if ...

… you don't like getting muddy or smelly.

CHAPTER 5

The Phenomenal Punkin' Chunkin' World Championship

What's the most obvious thing to do with your pumpkin after Halloween?

Hurl it in the air with a massive machine, of course!

That's the sport of Punkin' Chunkin'. It's probably called "Punkin' Chunkin'" and not Pumpkin Chucking because it rhymes better.

Where are the competitions?

Punkin' Chunkin' competitions take place all over the US, from Alabama to Wisconsin, every autumn, to help get rid of the pumpkin **surplus** after Halloween. At these festivals, people hurl pumpkins into the air and see how far they travel. The festivals often also offer fairground rides, dances, bouncy castles and pumpkin pie contests.

The biggest of all these festivals is the World Championships, where a hundred teams get together for the three-day festival. This used to be run in Tennessee, but the organisers are currently looking for a new home. However, it's not at all easy to find a good place to hold a Punkin' Chunkin' contest.

You see, Punkin' Chunkin' isn't just throwing a pumpkin into the air with your bare hands. If competitors want to break a world record, they need the pumpkin to travel kilometres. An average pumpkin festival involves throwing pumpkins over the length of a field. At the World Championships, the pumpkins can travel for 1.6 kilometres (nearly a mile), so they need a *huge*, empty space. That's why it's difficult for the World Championships to find a new home!

an ideal spot to fire pumpkins

The competitors use serious machines, like these!

How does it work?

Teams have to shoot a pumpkin out of
a machine. Some of these machines are simple
and made out of junk. Some of them are
massively complicated and expensive!

Each team has pumpkin spotters. They use
binoculars to follow the path of the pumpkin,
and then get on quad bikes to find out exactly
where they landed. When they have found
the place where the pumpkin has smashed
into the ground, they mark the spot with
spray paint. An independent judge then works
out the distance the pumpkin has travelled.

What are the rules?

Pumpkins must be shot into the air with a mechanical device.

Explosives are not allowed.

Pumpkins that burst in mid-air are called "pie" – short for "pumpkin pie in the sky".

Any pumpkins that burst like this are **disqualified**. (Poor pumpkins.)

How do the machines work?

There are lots of different sorts of machines.
Many of them use catapults.

A catapult is like a lever.

The competitors put the pumpkin in a sling.
It's pulled down with great force by ropes
or springs. Then they let go and the pumpkin
flies into the air!

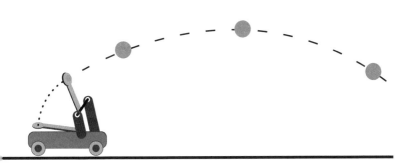

Punkin' chunkin' catapults work like this ...
but are just a bit bigger!

Some machines are powered by people!
These work a bit like a catapult as well.
The throwing arm is pulled back, not by
springs, but by a person cycling on a big wheel,
or a bicycle which is linked to the machine.

Air cannons use compressed air to shoot out
the pumpkin. These machines are the biggest
and most expensive.

The team put the pumpkin into the barrel
of the air cannon. Then they pull a lever.
All the air in the tanks shoots into the cannon,
and the pumpkin blasts off!

What makes a pumpkin travel the furthest?

How far a pumpkin travels depends on many factors, including:

- the weather (warm, dry air means they go faster and further!)
- where the machine is placed
- the sort of pumpkin – varieties such as Estrella and Lumina work best, as they have thicker rinds
- the size of the pumpkin (it must weigh between 3.6–4.5 kg, but the heavier pumpkins travel further).

Not to be tried if ...

... you don't own an enormous pumpkin shooter.

CHAPTER 6

The Best-Ever Bed Race

If you want to take part in the Great Bed Race, you need to prepare yourself for going on a bumpy race through a small town. Be warned, though – you'll end up splashing into a river!

You're in for a wild ride!

Do competitors use their actual beds?

No! They don't use actual beds. They use something that looks a bit like a bed. It's a big trolley on wheels, with poles and ropes for the runners to grab onto.

There are also usually about 30,000 people watching and cheering and the race is fast, so there's no time for snoozing. But there has to be someone in the "bed", and they have to hold on tight and not fall off!

When did it start?

The Bed Race takes place in a small town near York, in the north of England, every June.
It started in 1966, and similar events are held in the US, Germany and New Zealand.

There are 90 teams who race through the small town.

In each team, there are:

- six runners

- one passenger – often a child

- one bed.

What happens?

There's a whole day of fun and it's a party for the whole town.

At the start of the day, the teams and their beds look fantastic in fancy dress. Everyone makes a real effort! The beds are covered in layers of costume. There's a theme every year. In 2022, it was: The Environment: Reduce, Reuse, Recycle.

At 11 o'clock, the teams all gather at the local castle, and prizes are awarded for the Best-Dressed Bed and the Most Entertaining Team.

At 1 o'clock, the teams parade through the streets in all their finery. They're accompanied by marching bands and dance groups, and people cheer them through the town.

It's like a big carnival!

At 3 o'clock, the teams get changed and take the decorations off the bed.

Then the actual race begins. It all starts in a big field just outside the town centre.

Anyone can enter the bed race, but there's a maximum of 90 teams. That means there are 630 people running around the town! The teams set off, with the fastest going first. There are gaps of ten seconds in between the teams.

Fact!

In 2022, the fastest team took just under 13 minutes to complete the race successfully. That's very fast for a long race and a swim! The slowest team took 29 minutes – which is still very impressive! The race is 3.8 kilometres long.

Where does the race go?

The teams run through the **cobbled** streets of the town.

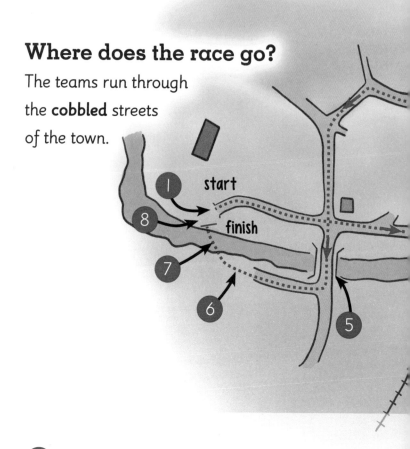

1 They start up a very steep hill,

2 then go up a big hill by the castle,

3 in and out of lots of bumpy cobbled streets,

4 and hurtle down the High Street.

5 Then they cross over a bridge

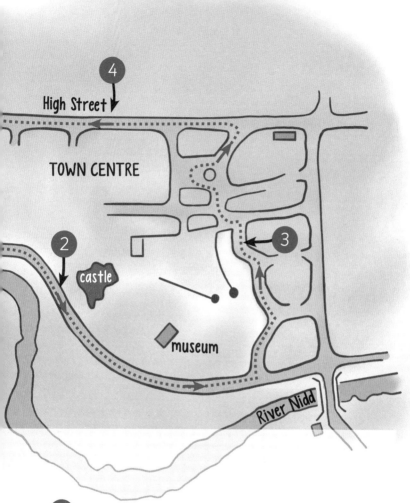

6 go through a woodland park,

7 cross the river,

8 and go back to the field where they started.

The fastest teams receive prizes. There are categories for men, women and mixed teams of men and women. There are also prizes for juniors aged 12–16.

One of the most popular places to watch the race is by the river.

This is the River Nidd. It's always cold and muddy, whatever the weather.

It's very slippery getting a bed on wheels out of the river – as you might expect!

Sometimes the beds capsize!

What if it rains?

Even if the weather is dreadful, the race goes ahead. The only time it has been cancelled was during the COVID-19 pandemic.

It's all done for charity, and it's a wonderful day out for the whole town.

Not to be tried if ...

... you don't like getting wet.

Bonus

The Great Bed Race

front cover of the guide for 2019

GREAT KNARESBOROUGH
BED RACE
SATURDAY 8TH JUNE 2019 | YORKSHIRE THEME

£2
ADULT
ADMISSION

the race

medal ceremony

medal

63

Bonus

Design your own championship

Now you've read about all the quirky and wonderful championships around the world, why not try making up your own contest?

Thing to be used/thrown/ eaten/chased, and so on!

food
(e.g. eggs, sweets, vegetables, cakes, cereal, porridge ...)

toys
(e.g. teddy bears, balls, cars, trains ...)

Category

smallest, tastiest, coolest, grooviest, fastest, furthest, heaviest, lightest, cleanest, muddiest, most colourful, biggest ...

Action

jumping, running, swimming, throwing, cooking, eating, chasing, balancing ...

Machine

scooter, bike, space hopper, balloon, water gun ...

65

When you've chosen ...

Now, mix them all together. What do you end up with?

You could have …

The Tastiest Cake Balancing Championships

The Muddiest Scooter-Racing Championship

The Wettest Water Gun Chasing Competition

The Cleanest Vegetable Throwing Competition

The Largest Bubble Gum Bubble Competition

Think ... is it a competition you could actually do? If so, remember ... your contest must be SAFE and NOT HURT ANYONE!

But if it's just in your imagination ... let your mind run free! You can make up ideas that simply sound funny! The stranger and the more fun the better! In fact, I bet that's how some of these other World Championships began ...

Glossary

accessible   easy to use

acoustic   a musical instrument which is not powered by electricity

cobbled   a surface made of stones

contestants   people taking part in competitions

championships   competitions to decide who is the best at doing something

decompose   to come apart

disqualified   taken out of a competition

fertile   producing lots of vegetation or crops

habitat   a place where animals and plants live

improvisation   creating something without rehearsing or thinking about it beforehand

jury a group of people who decide who wins a contest

Olympics the world's leading sporting events

optional leaving something as your own choice

perseverance to be able to keep on going

propel to move forward

rehearse to practise

surplus left over

symbolise to represent something

About the author

A bit about me ...

I love writing. I particularly love going into schools, libraries and bookshops to read my books and inspire children to write their own books. In my spare time, I love gardening and running. I also perform in local theatre shows (especially pantomimes), and sing with a band called *The Hot Crumpets*.

Teresa Heapy

How did you get into writing?

My dad, Ron Heapy, inspired me to make children's books. He was a brilliant children's book editor, and when I was little, he'd come home from work waving his books in the air. He'd encourage me and my brother to say what we thought of them, and sometimes asked us to help rewrite them.

What do you hope readers will get out of the book?

I hope readers get a sense of some of the amazing championships around the world, and the people who take part in them. What I found most encouraging as I researched the book was the passion and commitment of all the competitors.

Is there anything in this book that relates to your own experiences?

I like running, and I've run the Oxford Half Marathon race a few times. I like the challenge of pushing myself to run a long way, and the amazing sight of all the spectators cheering us on gives me tingles up and down my spine. That sense of togetherness and challenge, while raising money for a good cause, really appeals to me.

If you could enter any of the contests in this book, which would you choose?

The Cheese Roll race and the Tarragona towers fascinate me and terrify me – I wouldn't be brave enough to take part in either of those! I enjoy performing on stage, so I'd give the Air Guitar Championships a go (though I'm sure my children would be very embarrassed!). But because I love running, I think the Bed Race would be my number-one choice. It sounds like a brilliant day out with loads of fancy dress!

Why did you want to write this book?

I was strolling through a cold, boggy, wetland with my family one day, when my sister-in-law mentioned that there was a sport called bogsnorkelling. Bogsnorkelling? Really?! I looked it up, and was instantly inspired, both by the competition and the people doing it. There had to be more unusual sports, out there, didn't there ...?

Book chat

Had you heard of any of these competitions before reading the book?

Why do you think the book is called *Bed Races and Cheese Chases*?

If you could give the book a new title, what would you choose?

Which do you think is the best competition? Why?

Have you ever seen any of these competitions? Would you like to?

Why do you think people take part in competitions like these?

Would you like to try any of the competitions in this book? Which one and why?

What was the most interesting thing you learned from this book?

If you could talk to a competitor from any event, what would you ask them?

If you could ask the author one question, what would it be?

How important do you think the pictures are in the book?

Are there any competitions that you've heard of that aren't in the book?

Would you like to read about more quirky competitions?

Would you recommend this book? Why or why not?

Book challenge:
Design a medal for the competition you liked best.

Collins
BIG CAT

Published by Collins
An imprint of HarperCollins*Publishers*

The News Building
1 London Bridge Street
London SE1 9GF
UK

Macken House
39/40 Mayor Street Upper
Dublin 1
D01 C9W8
Ireland

10 9 8 7 6

ISBN 978-0-00-862465-1

British Library Cataloguing-in-Publication
Data
A catalogue record for this publication is
available from the British Library.

Download the teaching notes and
word cards to accompany this book at:
http://littlewandle.org.uk/signupfluency/

Get the latest Collins Big Cat news at
collins.co.uk/collinsbigcat

Author: Teresa Heapy
Publisher: Lizzie Catford
Product manager: Caroline Green
Series editor: Charlotte Raby
Commissioning editor: Suzannah Ditchburn
Development editor: Catherine Baker
Project manager: Emily Hooton
Content editor: Daniela Mora Chavarría
Copyeditor: Catherine Dakin
Phonics reviewer: Rachel Russ
Proofreader: Gaynor Spry
Photo researcher: Charlie Hooton
Cover designer: Sarah Finan
Typesetter: 2Hoots Publishing Services Ltd
Production controller: Katharine Willard

Collins would like to thank the teachers and children at the
following schools who took part in the trialling of Big Cat
for Little Wandle Fluency: Burley And Woodhead Church of
England Primary School; Chesterton Primary School; Lady
Margaret Primary School; Little Sutton Primary School;
Parsloes Primary School.

Printed and bound in the UK

MIX
Paper | Supporting
responsible forestry
FSC™ C007454

This book contains FSC™ certified paper and other controlled
sources to ensure responsible forest management.

For more information visit: www.harpercollins.co.uk/green

Acknowledgements
The publishers gratefully acknowledge the permission
granted to reproduce the copyright material in this book.
Every effort has been made to trace copyright holders and to
obtain their permission for the use of copyright material. The
publishers will gladly receive any information enabling them
to rectify any error or omission at the first opportunity.

p3 Colin Underhill/Alamy, p7 Frederic Reglain/Alamy, p10
Lucas Vallecillos/Alamy, p11 jordi clave garsot/Alamy, p15
Lucas Vallecillos/Alamy, p17 Elizabeth Emmerson/Alamy,
p18 Rob Lacey/Alamy, p19 Mary Evans Picture Library,
p20 PA Images/Alamy, p21 Adrian Dennis/Getty Images,
p22 horst friedrichs/Alamy, p23 Mark Hawkins/Alamy,
p24 Stephen Shepherd/Alamy, p25 Mikal Ludlow/Alamy,
pp27tr, p27bl, p29 & p34 courtesy of the Air Guitar World
Championships/Sirja Majaluoto, p30 Eeva Riihela/Getty
Images, p37 & p43 courtesy of the World Bogsnorkelling
Championships/Peter Barnett, p38 robertharding/Alamy, p40
Adrian Sherratt/Alamy, p42t Peter Lane/Alamy, p42b Peter
Lane/Alamy, p47 Associated Press/Alamy, p48 Associated
Press/Alamy, p50 Dennis Brack/Alamy, pp52–56 & p62
courtesy of Knaresborough Lions Club, p60 RHB/Alamy, p61
PA Images/Alamy; all other photographs Shutterstock.